srsly
Hamlet

more OMG shakespeare!

YOLO Juliet

srsly Hamlet

william shakespeare

+

courtney carbone

Random House 🏠 New York

To all my extraordinary English teachers,
I'm sorry. 📚
—C.B.C.

Text copyright © 2015 by Random House LLC

Emoji copyright © Apple Inc.

Image on page 6 copyright © Shutterstock/André Klaassen, page 59 copyright
© GettyImages/Photodisc, page 60 copyright © iStock/manwolste,
page 60 © Shutterstock/Fernanado Cortes, both images on page 95
© GettyImages/PhotoAlto/Milena Boniek, page 99 © GettyImages/donald_gruener

Visit us on the Web! randomhouseteens.com

Educators and librarians, for a variety of teaching tools,
visit us at RHTeachersLibrarians.com

Library of Congress Cataloging-in-Publication Data
Carbone, Courtney.
Srsly Hamlet / William Shakespeare and Courtney Carbone. — First edition.
pages cm.
Summary: "William Shakespeare's tragedy told in the style of texts, tweets,
and status posts." —Provided by publisher
ISBN 978-0-553-53538-9 (trade) — ISBN 978-0-553-53547-1 (ebook)
[1. Shakespeare, William, 1564–1616—Adaptations.] I. Shakespeare, William, 1564–1616.
Hamlet. II. Title. III. Title: Seriously Hamlet. IV. Title: Hamlet.
PZ7.C1863Sr 2015 [Fic]—dc23 2014041937

MANUFACTURED IN CHINA
10 9 8 7 6 5 4 3 2 1
First Edition

who's who

 Hamlet, Prince of Denmark

 The Ghost, Hamlet's dead dad, the old King Hamlet

 Queen Gertrude, Hamlet's mom, now married
to Claudius

 King Claudius, Hamlet's dad's brother, Hamlet's
uncle *and* stepdad

 Ophelia

 Laertes, Ophelia's brother

 Polonius, Ophelia and Laertes's father, councillor
to King Claudius

 Reynaldo, servant to Polonius

 Horatio, Hamlet's friend

 Voltimand, member of the Danish court

 Cornelius, member of the Danish court

Send

who's who (cont.)

 Rosencrantz, member of the Danish court, Hamlet's old friend

 Guildenstern, member of the Danish court, Hamlet's old friend

 Francisco, Danish soldier

 Bernardo, Danish soldier

 Marcellus, Danish soldier

 Fortinbras, Prince of Norway

 Gravedigger

 Angry Mob

characters you won't meet in this book

(aka people w/o smartphones)

 Osric, member of the Danish court

 Gentlemen

 A Lord

 A Captain in Fortinbras's army

 Ambassadors to Denmark from England

 Players who take the roles of Prologue, Player King, Player Queen, and Lucianus in *The Murder of Gonzago*

 Two Messengers

 Sailors

 Gravedigger's companion

 Doctor of Divinity

 Attendants, Lords, Guards, Musicians, Laertes's Followers, Soldiers, Officers

Send

srsly
Hamlet

💀

Act 1

[Scene 1]

Bernardo

almost there!! 😅

Francisco

Who is this?

Bernardo

sry new #

Francisco

Bernardo?

Bernardo

yep. it's after 🕐 . go 2 bed!! i'll take over.

Francisco

Thx, yeah I'm super 😴.

Bernardo

lmk if you 👀 horatio or marcellus. they're on 💂 ⏱ 2nite 2.

Francisco

K

Send

Group text: Marcellus, Bernardo, Horatio

Marcellus

> BRB. Bringing Horatio so he can c u-know-who. 😏

Bernardo

> the 👻?

Marcellus

> Yup

Horatio

> IF this 👻 is real, it's 👎 4 Denmark.

> BTW did you guys see the I posted this morning?
> www.NorwegianNews.com/article/Norway-Pretending-It-Won-War-Against-Denmark/

Marcellus

> TL;DR. Can I get a recap??

Horatio

> The late King Hamlet won a war against Norway's late King Fortinbras, yes?

Send

Bernardo

yeah, i know . . . but what were they late 4?

Horatio

SMH. That means dead. 😵

Bernardo

ah . . .

Horatio

Anyway, King Hamlet defeated King Fortinbras fair and ⬛ , but his son, Prince Fortinbras, is threatening to attack us to avenge his father's death. ⏳ 💣

Bernardo

that can't be good.

Marcellus

Horatio

Speaking of which, when is this 👻 supposed to show? It's ❄️ out here!

Send

Bernardo

yesterday he showed rite after the 🔔 . . .
kinda like the 1 ringing now . . .

Marcellus

OMG! Did you c that?!

#NoFilter

Bernardo

holy 💩 !! it looks like a 👻 of the 😵 king!

Marcellus

Well, what do u have 2 say now, Horatio?

Horatio

Man. You were right. 🙈

Send

marcellus

And u were . . . ?? Remind me. I forget! 😉

Horatio

😒 Relax. What do we do now?

marcellus

 it?

Bernardo

stab a 👻? u can't kill something that's already 😵 !!

Horatio

Too late! It's gone. We have to tell Hamlet asap.

Bernardo

you're rite. the 👻 will want 2 talk 2 his son.

[Scene 2]

 Claudius
RIP @KingHamlet. You'll b missed.

 [REPLY]

Send

Claudius
And now that funeral is over, let's get on w/ the wedding! 😭 / 😄 Shout-out 2 my beautiful , @Gertrude. #blessed

👍 Gertrude likes this.

REPLY

Hamlet: Srsly?

Group text: Claudius, Voltimand, Cornelius

claudius

I need u guys. 🙏

voltimand

What's up?

claudius

Did you c the link Horatio posted?

cornelius

Yeah, everyone's been talking about it.

Send

claudius

K well I didn't read the whole 📰 , but it sounds like I need ppl 2 go 2 Norway, talk w/ Fortinbras's uncle, and convince him to keep his 👨‍👩‍👦 from attacking us. Can u do that 4 me?

voltimand

Yeah, np.

cornelius

We'll catch the next ⛵ .

claudius

Thx. I'd do it myself but I have my 🎉 2nite. 😜

+ i'm the king 🙌

Group text: Laertes, Claudius, Polonius

Laertes

Your 👑 ness, I have something 2 ask of u.

claudius

Yes?

Send

Laertes

It's been gr8 seeing u 👑 and everything, but now that it's over, I'd like 2 go back 2 school 🏫 in France.

claudius

Polonius, wut do u think? Laertes

polonius

👌 by me.

claudius

Laertes, u r free 2 go. Ttyl. 👋

Group text: Claudius, Hamlet, Gertrude

claudius

Hamlet, my nephew/new son! Wut's new?

Hamlet

That about covers it.

claudius

Something wrong? Why is ur head still ?

Send

Hamlet

Actually, I am too much in the ☀️. I can't believe you people are 💑 like nothing happened.

Gertrude

Son, I wish you would 😃. It's common to 😭. But everything that lives must 😵 eventually.

Hamlet

Common is one word for it.

Gertrude

Why do you seem to take it to 🖤 ?

Hamlet

Seem? No, Mother. I don't SEEM 😠. I AM 😠.

Claudius

Hamlet, really, it's been 2 months already 📅 📅 ! Move on! Look @ ur mother. She's already remarried! 💒 Parents 😵 all the ⏰. I'm ur father now. Deal. 1 day you'll be king just like me!!! 🎉 !

Send

🍵 help me. God, I want to 😵. I wish I could 😵 and not go to 🔥😈 for killing myself. My dad hasn't even been 😵 two months, and already everyone has forgotten about him. He was such an amazing 👑, and he gets replaced by my 💩 uncle.

Does no one remember how good my father was to my mother? 💐💝😍 I wish I didn't have to 💭 about it. She was 🖤🖤🖤 with him. And yet 2 📅 s later she has completely moved on. How is that possible?? Even 🐴🐟🐱🐷 are more loyal than that. And not only does she move on, she MARRIES 💍 my father's brother. My UNCLE. Who is the complete and total OPPOSITE of my father. Her 💧👠 were barely dry by the wedding. It's too much too fast. (Also, kind of INCEST. Just saying.)

It's bad. And I know it will only get worse. And yet . . . as I am, there's nothing I can do.

● ● ●

Horatio

Hey, stranger.

Hamlet

Horatio! Great to hear from you! 😃

Horatio

Listen, I heard about your father. I'm so, so sorry. I'm in the to pay my respects.

Hamlet

Ha! More like you got an invite to my mother's 👰.

Horatio

SMH, one did quickly follow the other.

Send

Hamlet

#understatement

I'm pretty sure they used the same 🍗 🍰 🍷 for both.

You know, sometimes I think I still 👀 my father. Just can't believe he's gone. 😔

Horatio

Funny you should 💬 that.

Hamlet

?

Horatio

I think I saw him last night IRL.

Hamlet

⁉️

Horatio

This is going to sound 🌀, but long 📖 short, Marcellus and Bernardo saw his 👻 while on ⏰. They asked me to come 👀 for myself.

Send

On the third night, I went. Swear to God . . . 👻 was real.

Hamlet

⚠️ I don't know what to say.

Are you going back <u>tonight</u>?

Horatio

Yes.

Hamlet

How did he look?

Horatio

More 🙁 than 😬.

Hamlet

😠 or 😌 ?

Horatio

😠

Hamlet

I'll go with you <u>tonight</u>. Maybe he'll come back.

Send

Horatio

I think he will.

Hamlet

The way I feel right now, the 😈 couldn't keep me from talking to him.

Let's keep this between us. 😶

Horatio

🙈🙊🙉 See you later.

Hamlet

I'll be there before <u>midnight</u>.

[Scene 3]

Laertes

Hey, sis, my 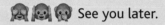 is here. Don't want 2 miss my ⛵ 2 🇫🇷. I'm going 2 miss you so much. Promise me you'll ?

Ophelia

don't be silly. of course i will!

Send

Laertes

And listen . . . there's something else I want 2 talk 2 u about.

ophelia

your excessive use of 2s???

Laertes

Ha. Ha. Ha. 😑

ophelia

i'm listening. . . .

Laertes

I know u have been hanging out w/ Hamlet a lot lately. I just want 2 make sure you're not getting 😍. Sure he might say he 🖤 u now. But he's the prince. 🤴 His #1 priority is & always will b 👑. Please just don't get 😫.

ophelia

i know, i know. you have nothing to worry about.

Laertes

So you'll b careful?

Send

ophelia

i have 🔓 your words in my 💜 and you alone have the 🔑. but it goes both ways. you better stay out of trouble in 📖 !

Laertes

👍

polonius

Son, b4 u go, I made this 📄 for u.

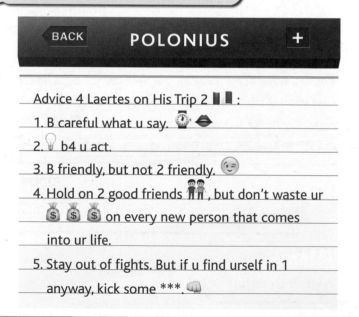

BACK | **POLONIUS** | **+**

Advice 4 Laertes on His Trip 2 📖 :

1. B careful what u say. ⌚ 👄
2. 💡 b4 u act.
3. B friendly, but not 2 friendly. 😉
4. Hold on 2 good friends 👬, but don't waste ur 💰 💰 💰 on every new person that comes into ur life.
5. Stay out of fights. But if u find urself in 1 anyway, kick some ***. 👊

Send

6. Listen 2 every1, but don't waste ⏰ & energy on ppl who don't deserve it.

7. 👀 what other ppl do, but don't 👮 them.

8. Dress nicely, but don't go overboard. (u know how 🎽🎽 ppl are.) 🎩 💰 💼 🔪

9. Don't borrow or lend 💲 2 friends or u might lose both. And/or u might start 2 resent them. And/or they might start 2 resent u! 😠

10. Above all: b true 2 urself. If u are completely urself, then u 🚫 b fake 2 any1!! ☆

Laertes

Thx, Dad. I'll let u know when I get there. 😎

Polonius

Good luck! 🍀

Group text: Laertes, Ophelia, Polonius

Laertes

About 2 board. Bye, guys. Ophelia, remember wut I said!! 🔓

Send

ophelia

xoxo

● ● ●

polonius

U can tell me what that was about when I get 🏠.

ophelia

sigh. if you must know, it was about hamlet.

polonius

I knew it. U 2 have been spending a lot of ⏰ 2gether. What's going on? & ⚠️ don't u dare lie 2 me!

ophelia

dad, it's just . . .

he 💘 me.

polonius

He probably 💘 CANOODLING w/ u!

Send

ophelia

ew. dad. please don't ever say something like that again.

polonius

Don't b naïve. He's the prince! Do I need 2 make U a  of advice like ur brother?! That's it. U r forbidden 2 speak 2 Hamlet ever again. 😕

ophelia

dad, stop. you're overreacting. he's serious about me. 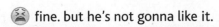 soon?? 😉

polonius

You rly don't have a choice. This ends NOW, Ophelia.

ophelia

😫 fine. but he's not gonna like it.

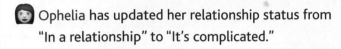 Ophelia has updated her relationship status from "In a relationship" to "It's complicated."

👍   REPLY

Send

[Scene 4]

Claudius has posted 11 new photos to the album:
<u>Here We Go a-Wassailing!</u> —with <u>Queen Gertrude</u>
and <u>10 others</u>.

👍 Queen Gertrude likes this.
REPLY

Hamlet
It's almost <u>midnight</u>. LET'S DO THIS. #FOMO
👍
REPLY

Group text: Marcellus, Hamlet, Horatio

marcellus

Where u @?!

Hamlet

On the way to the gate.

Horatio

Almost there.

marcellus

K. What's all that coming from the ?

Send

Hamlet

Don't remind me. My uncle is getting .

Marcellus

Srsly? Kings still do that on their wedding nite??

Hamlet

Not the good ones. FML.

Marcellus

Look out!! I think I see the 👻!

Hamlet

I see it, too! It wants me to follow him!

Horatio

NO. It's too dangerous.

Hamlet

What's the worst that could happen? I DIE? Have u forgotten how much my life sucks right now? 😖

Send

Horatio

STOP. Hamlet, please.

Hamlet

Another word and I'll you, Horatio. I swear to God.

Horatio

😞

> Marcellus
> Something is 💩 in the state of Denmark.
>
>   REPLY

[Scene 5]

✅ Hamlet and Ghost of Hamlet have checked into Creepy Black Forest.

Ghost

Hamlet, I don't have much ⏰, but I must tell you a terrible 📖, and ask for your help in avenging my MURDER.

Hamlet

MURDER?!

Send

Ghost

Yes, MURDER. While I was 😴 in the 🍎🌳🍎🌳, a 🐍 stung me. And that 🐍 now wears my 👑.

Hamlet

I knew it! Uncle-Dad Claudius! 😫

Ghost

Yes. That wicked 🐀 took my life, my 🏰, my 👑, my 👰 —everything!

Hamlet

How???

Ghost

While I was 😴, 🧔 poured some ⚡ into my 👂. Poison! 💉 I never had a chance. If you ever really 💚ed me, you will 🏃 2 🔪🧔.

Hamlet

Of course I will! Um 😬, what about Aunt-Mom?

Send

Ghost

> It's not up to us to punish her. Leave her to the 👮👮.
> Now I have to go. Good-bye, Hamlet. 👋 Remember me.

Hamlet

> You have my word. Revenge is all I can think
> about now. I swear ✋ it will be done.

Group text: Horatio, Marcellus, Hamlet

Horatio

> Hamlet, where did you go?

Marcellus

> Everything OK?!

Hamlet

> Yes, but promise never to repeat ANYTHING
> that happened tonight.

Marcellus

> I sweat!

Send

Horatio

I sweat, too!

Marcellus

*swear lolz #DamnYouAutocomplete

Hamlet

Guys, this is serious. 😒

Marcellus

Sry, sry. I swear!

Horatio

Me too. 👍

Hamlet

Good. Cut & paste that a few more times so I know you mean it.

Horatio

I swear! I swear! I swear!

Marcellus

I swear! I swear! I swear!

Send

Marcellus

R we good? I don't have unlimited txts.

Hamlet

Okay, but listen—and this is important—from now on, I will be acting . You guys have to go along with it. Okay?

Marcellus

K

Horatio

👍

Send

Act 2

[Scene 1]

Polonius

> I need u 2 keep close ⌚ on my son.

Reynaldo

> What 4, boss?

Polonius

> He's going off 2 🏢, and u know what that means.

Reynaldo

> A lifetime of student loans? 📪 💸

Polonius

> No! I'm worried he'll b 🍺 👊 🎱 🐎 💃 !

Reynaldo

> I see. And how would you like me to find out?

Polonius

> Tell people he's been 🍺 👊 🎱 🐎 💃 !

Send

Reynaldo

Huh?

Polonius

If u that he does & other people agree, then we'll know he does! 😉

Reynaldo

don't u think that will give him a bad reputation? IMHO

Polonius

Just make it seem like NBD. He's young! He's free! We'll use lies 2 find out the truth. Get it now?

Reynaldo

Whatever u say, boss. 👍

ophelia

dad! help! i need you!!!!!!!!!

Polonius

What's wrong?

Send

ophelia

it's hamlet. he stormed into my room looking like he'd seen a 👻 and rambled like a 🌀 person!!! then he just 👀 at me and walked out the 🚪 again!!!!!!

polonius

👂 like he's lost his mind. Did u do anything 2 make him 😠 ?

ophelia

only EXACTLY what YOU told me to do!!! not txt him or respond to his txts.

polonius

That must b it. He's gone 🌀 bc he 😍 u. I'll tell the king at once. Brb.

[Scene 2]

✅ Rosencrantz and Guildenstern have checked into Elsinore Castle—with Queen Gertrude and King Claudius.

Send

Group text: Gertrude, Guildenstern, Claudius, Rosencrantz

gertrude

Welcome! I'm so 😃 you made it to the 🏛 safely. Meet us in the lobby?

guildenstern

Of course! B right there.

claudius

And thx again for offering 2 talk 2 Hamlet.

rosencrantz

Happy 2 help. Hopefully we'll get 2 the bottom of this. 😟

gertrude

If his two BFFs can't get through to him, IDK what will.

guildenstern

Wish us !

● ● ●

📬 Welcome, Gertrude! You have 10 new messages from Polonius waiting in folder: Spam.

Send

claudius

Did u c all the ✉ Polonius sent? He said they r 💜 from Hamlet 2 Ophelia.

gertrude

Nope. I forward everything from Polonius to my spam folder. 😉

claudius

He thinks he 👃 wut's wrong w/ Hamlet.

gertrude

Besides the fact that his father is dead and I just married you?

claudius

Yeah, Polonius thinks Hamlet 💝 Ophelia. U think that could b it?

gertrude

Only one way to 🔍 out the truth.

📬 Welcome, Claudius! You have received an e-card from Voltimand and Cornelius.

Send

Good news! We talked 2 Fortinbras's uncle, Old Norway, and he said he is willing 2 attack Poland instead of us! Looks like we're safe 4 now. Denmark FTW!

Group text: Claudius, Polonius, Gertrude

claudius

Polonius, can u PROVE that Hamlet is 😭 bc he 💜 Ophelia?

polonius

Let's have her reach out 2 him and 👀 what happens. I'll text him 2.

● ● ●

polonius

Hello. How r u?

Hamlet

Fine, thx.

Send

polonius

> U know who this is, rite?

Hamlet

> Yes, of course. You're a !

polonius

> No, u must b thinking of sum1 else.

Hamlet

> Well, I wish you were a because at least those guys are honest.

polonius

> IDK what u r talking about.

Hamlet

> Do you have a daughter? 🧑

polonius

> U know that I do.

Hamlet

> Watch out for her. It's a 🌀 dangerous 🌍 we live in.

Send

Polonius

Tru 😔 . . . uh, so what r u up 2?

Hamlet

Reading.

Polonius

What are you reading?

Hamlet

📕 📘 📕

Polonius

But what r the 📚 about?

Hamlet

About a 🌀 old fool! 🐵 Imagine that! Srsly, an 🐵
can become a 👶 if like a crab u go backward.

Polonius

Ah. Well, I guess I should let u go.

Hamlet

I guess you should.

Send

Polonius

Not gonna name names, but there's a method 2 a CERTAIN someone's madness.

REPLY

Group text: Rosencrantz, Guildenstern, Hamlet

ROSENCRANTZ

Guess what?

GUILDENSTERN

R&G in the 🏠!

HAMLET

You came to see me in ?

ROSENCRANTZ

You're on fire?!?!

HAMLET

No, no. Hell. Why are you here?

ROSENCRANTZ

We wanted 2 see u.

Send

Hamlet

Ah, so no one MADE you come?

Rosencrantz

No.

Guildenstern

Yes.

I mean no?

Rosencrantz

I mean yes?

Hamlet

SMH you two need to get your 📖 straight.

Rosencrantz

●●●

Guildenstern

●●●

Hamlet

Just FYI: I'm depressed. Life is supposed to be s and ☀️ but right now I don't feel anything. 😑

Send

Rosencrantz

That sux, but we have a that might cheer u up.

Hamlet

What's that?

Guildenstern

A !

Rosencrantz

We brought a bunch of actors from the .

Hamlet

Oh yeah? Can I pick the ?

Guildenstern

Of course, if it will make u feel better. 😃

Hamlet

Oh, it most certainly will. 😏

📥 Hamlet has added 1 script for the play *The Murder of Gonzago* and 1 Wite-Out bottle to cart.

Send

Act 3

[Scene 1]

◀ BACK **HAMLET** ✚

2 🐝 or 🚫 2 🐝, that is the ❓. Is it better to muddle through a miserable life you have no control over? Or is it better to 👊 back and maybe win? If I died—if I gave up and threw in the towel—all my problems would go away. I'd have no more 💧💧 or 💔.

But 😵 could be even worse than life! WTF. Maybe it's better to deal with the problems I have than end up with others that are WORSE? That's the thing, isn't it? We're all cowards because we don't know what comes next. So we muddle through, and don't do anything for fear of making things worse. #TheStruggleIsReal

claudius

> I think u should have Ophelia talk 2 Hamlet. Then we can 👀 the txts and decide wut 2 do.

Send

polonius

K stay tuned!

☑ Hamlet has checked into the Elsinore Castle Lobby.

Hamlet

Hi.

ophelia

how are you?

Hamlet

Been better.

ophelia

we need to talk. i have to give you back all the 💌 you wrote me.

Hamlet

I never wrote you any 💌.

Send

ophelia

don't make this harder than it has to be. you know you did. and they were beautiful and appreciated, but i can't keep them. it's just not working out. 👩

hamlet?

SAY SOMETHING!

Hamlet

What do you want me to say?

ophelia

i don't know. SOMETHING.

Hamlet

You know, I really did 💙 you.

ophelia

.i know.

Hamlet

And yet I didn't 💙 you at all.

Send

ophelia

????

Hamlet

Look. Just give up on 👫 💚 and join the 🏛️. IMHO all 🚹 are terrible, and the last thing you need is to start a 👨‍👩‍👧 in this wretched 🌍. I don't get it. 🚺 dress up and dumb down. and 👶 talk. It's all so fake. I'M SICK OF IT.

ophelia

wow. tell me how you really feel.

Hamlet

 GO.

👩 Ophelia

💔 Ophelia has changed her relationship status from "It's complicated" to "Single."

👍   REPLY

Horatio: Oh no, what happened?
Rosencrantz: Are you going to the show tonight?

Send

polonius

How did it go?

ophelia

you were right about hamlet. i have the txts to prove it.

polonius

I'll let the know. . . . .

🎵 Ophelia is listening to "Men Suck Breakup Mix."

Claudius

ness in great 1s must be watched.

👍

REPLY

Hamlet: Agreed.

[Scene 2]

Hamlet

Horatio, I need to talk to you.

Send

Horatio

What's up? The 🎭 is about to start and I want a good 💺.

Hamlet

It's about the 🎭! I had the cast add a scene of my own 📝, and I want you to watch the king's face when that part is acted out. 😇? 😏? 😰?

Horatio

What kind of scene?

Hamlet

Basically the murder of my father in the 🍎🌳🍎🌳. If my uncle looks guilty, we'll know that the 👻 was telling the truth. Claudius is a murderer! 😡

Horatio

Brilliant 💡. I'll keep my 👀 on him, and we'll meet up after to discuss.

Chat Server

Elsinore Castle Theater Presents:
The Murder of Gonzago REMIX

Claudius: Show ⏰! Every1 find ur seats.

Hamlet: The setup is taking too long. Can't they get on with it?

Ophelia: stop posting and pay attention. it'll be quick.

Hamlet: Quick as a certain mother's love?

Rosencrantz: I'll tell u what ur mother luvs. 😏

Horatio: Is it just me or does that actress look like the queen?

Gertrude: I don't see it. That actress complains too much. Probably lying. 👖 🔥

Polonius: I don't get what's going on. Some1 explain this 2 me!!!!!

Hamlet: The actress is confessing her 💜 for her husband and saying that if he dies, then she'll never remarry because that would be like him dying twice. Fidelity FTW.

Rosencrantz: Whoa. That totally went over my head. G?

Guildenstern: Yeah, I got nothing. 😑

Hamlet: Keep watching.

Polonius: OK I am lost again!! 2 bad this play doesn't come with a GPS. lolz

Send

Rosencrantz: ✋ Yah. Hamlet. A little help here??

Hamlet: Srsly? Very basic stuff, guys. The woman's husband was murdered by a villain while the husband was asleep in the orchard. The murderer poisoned him—then ended up with his 👑 and 👸!

Gertrude: Hamlet, have we seen this one before? #DejaVu

Claudius: STOP THE PLAY. SHUT IT DOWN.

Ophelia: what's going on? ☹️

Polonius: 🎭 is canceled! Everybody go 🏠!!

Guildenstern: WTF. should we 👏 ?

● ○ ●

Hamlet

Did you see what just happened?!

The 👻 was right! My uncle's 😨 when he heard "poison." ⚡

Horatio

Congrats? 🎉? What happens now?

Hamlet

Wait and 👀.

Send

Group text: Guildenstern, Hamlet, Rosencrantz

Guildenstern

> Hamlet, the 👑 wants 2 talk 2 u.

Rosencrantz

> I don't get u. We used to be 👬.

Hamlet

> We're still 👬!

Guildenstern

> So tell us why you're acting like this!!!!

Hamlet

> Send me a video of you playing a song. 🎵🎺

Guildenstern

> WTF. IDK how to play 🎺.

Hamlet

> It would mean a lot to me.

Guildenstern

> I couldn't even if I wanted 2.

Send

Hamlet

lol

Guildenstern

What's funny?

Hamlet

You don't know about 🎵 and you admit it. And yet you would play ME even though you know NOTHING about my situation. YOU THINK I'M SIMPLER TO UNDERSTAND THAN A 🎺 !!!

Guildenstern

Wow, it just got cold in here.

Rosencrantz

#shade

Polonius

The queen wants 2 c u asap.

Hamlet

✋ I'll go when I damn well please.

Send

polonius

I can say you better do it soon!

Hamlet

"You better do it soon" is easy to say. lolz

🚫 Polonius has been added to your "Blocked Caller" list

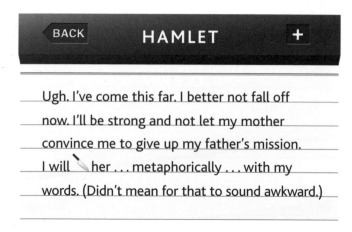

BACK **HAMLET** +

Ugh. I've come this far. I better not fall off now. I'll be strong and not let my mother convince me to give up my father's mission. I will ✎ her . . . metaphorically . . . with my words. (Didn't mean for that to sound awkward.)

[Scene 3]

Group text: Claudius, Guildenstern, Rosencrantz

claudius

I h8 that stupid kid! He's completely outta control!! I need 2 send him away. 😠 2 🇬🇧 !

Send

Guildenstern

Sending him away seems like the only option. You're the 👑. It's best 4 everybody 2 get him out of here.

Rosencrantz

We'll go w/ him.

Claudius

Please do. & hurry! 🏃

● ● ●

Polonius

My lord, Hamlet is going 2 swing by to see Gertrude. I'm gonna hide behind the drapes and watch what happens. 😈

I'll let u know how it goes b4 zzZ.

Claudius

Thx! 😃

Send

BACK **CLAUDIUS** +

I murdered my brother. Does that make me a terrible person? This is some Cain and Abel 💩 right here. I can't even 🙏, I feel so guilty. And at the same ⏰, I am still 😄 with the outcome! Is there nothing I can do 2 ever make up 4 my crime? Guess it doesn't rly matter. Wut's done is done. I can't change it n-e-way so I may as well enjoy it! My 👑, 👸🤵, etc. Things r looking 📈! So wut can I say? #SorryNotSorry

BACK **HAMLET** +

You'll never freaking believe this. I saw Claudius PRAYING today. In the ⛪. That 😈. PRAYING. 🙏 What am I supposed to do with that?! I thought about him right there, but that doesn't help me because if I kill him when he's "repenting," then he'll just

Send

go str8 to 🐱🐱🐱. Meanwhile he poisoned
MY father when he least suspected it. So
Dad didn't even get a chance to make up for
all the things he did wrong in his life. Now
he's basically in 🔥🔥🔥 forever (or
something . . . not sure how that works).

I will just have to wait to 🔪 Claudius the
next time he does something terrible. Which
shouldn't be long, considering his hobbies
consist of 🍺, 🎁 Mom, and 🔪 people. He
needs to go to hell where he belongs. 😈
#RoyalProblems

[Scene 4]

polonius

Hamlet's on his way. R u ready? Remember, tell him
ur 😴 of his games. I'm gonna hide.

gertrude

I know. We've been over this. Go!

Send

gertrude

Where are you?

Hamlet

Coming over. I heard you wanted to talk?

gertrude

Hurry up. Your father is really 😠 with you.

Hamlet

My father?! MY father is really 😠 with YOU!

gertrude

What's wrong?! I didn't raise you this way. Have you forgotten who I am? 😔

Hamlet

You're the QUEEN. 👑 Your husband's brother's wife! And my MOTHER (though I wish you weren't). ✖️ 👩‍👧‍👦

gertrude

Are you *trying* to make my 🖤 stop beating?

Send

Hamlet

Hold on. I'm here, but I heard a noise. . . .

Gertrude

What?

Hamlet

It's coming from . . .

INSIDE OUR HOUSE. 😱

Gertrude

I'm sure it's nothing.

Hamlet

BRB

Gertrude

Hamlet?

Where are you?

HAMLET?!?! Answer me!!

Send

Hamlet

Mom.

I just 🔪 someone.

Gertrude

WHAT?! 😧

Hamlet

Come over and help me. I'm scared to look. 🙁

Gertrude

You just KILLED someone?! That's bad. 👎

Hamlet

I guess it's almost as bad as, say, murdering a king and 💍 his wife.

Gertrude

!?

Hamlet

I said what I said.

💩

Send

Hamlet
Anyone know a good lawyer?

👍 REPLY

Hamlet

It was Polonius. That !

Gertrude

You killed Polonius?!

Hamlet

I thought it was the king! 👑 ARGH. Why did Polonius have to get involved?! Mom, listen to me. I need you to have a 🖤 here.

Gertrude

What have I done that is so, SO terrible that you won't forgive me?

Send

Hamlet

Mom. Look at this pic.

Look @ Dad. Look how royal and regal he is. He LOOKS like a true king because HE IS A TRUE KING. This was your husband.

Gertrude

Aw. I loved that outfit.

Hamlet

Now look @ Claudius.

Send

See how many filters he uses? You can't honestly tell me you're *attracted* to him. You're 👵 now! Not 🙋 and horny.

Gertrude

Watch it.

Hamlet

How could you do this, really? Marry a murderer who cheated his way to the 👑 ? It SICKENS me. 🤢 If there was an emoji for vomit, I'd send it to you. 📬

Gertrude

Hamlet. Please. 🙇 You're making me feel 😭.

Hamlet

I'm just telling you the truth, Mom. Think about where you zᶻᐟ at night.

Gertrude

HAMLET! STOP!

● ● ●

Send

ghost

Hamlet.

Hamlet

Oh, hey, Dad. Kinda in the middle of something.

ghost

Just checking in. Wanted to make sure you were following the plan. Remember, don't punish your mother.

● ● ●

Hamlet

Hold on. Just got a text from Dad. I'll send it to you.

Gertrude

Um . . . I don't see anything.

Hamlet

Let me try again.

Send

Gertrude

Nope.

Hamlet

How can you not see it?! IT'S DAD!!!

Gertrude

Hamlet, I understand you're upset. But it's all in your head. You're hallucinating. Getting txt messages from a dead man? That's 🌀 talk.

Is there anything you want to tell me? 💊 ILY no matter what.

Hamlet

NO. You just can't admit you did something wrong. So you're putting it on me. But it's not too late. ⌛ Dump Claudius. Make things right.

Gertrude

Hamlet, you've broken my 🖤 in two. 💔

Hamlet

Well, keep the good 1/2 and throw out the bad!

Send

Hamlet

. . . You still there?

Gertrude

Barely.

Hamlet

I'm going to 🇬🇧 tomorrow.

Gertrude

I almost forgot. Do you have 2?

Hamlet

Yeah, my 💳 has already been charged. Can't let down my "good friends" Rosencrantz & Guildenstern. Though it's probably not the worst thing for me to get out of the 🏰 for a while. Because Polonius. 😬

Moving the body now. G'night.

Send

Act 4

[Scene 1]

gertrude

> 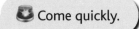 Come quickly.

claudius

> Wut's wrong? Everything OK?

gertrude

> I don't even know where to start.

claudius

> OIC. It's Hamlet, isn't it? What did he do now?

gertrude

> Long 📖 short, he's as 🌀 as ever. He heard Polonius spying on him and ✏️ him to death. 💀 So awful.

claudius

> OMG that could have been me!!

> He's outta control. We let him get away w/ everything 2 easy.

> Where is he now?

Send

gertrude

Getting rid of the body. You know, I think he actually feels bad about it. 😔

claudius

#NotMyProblem #ICouldCareLess

gertrude

You mean you couldn't care less.

claudius

Huh? We need 2 do serious damage control. ⚠️ ⚠️ ⚠️ Our only option is 2 get in front of this. That way it doesn't . . . wait 4 it . . . stab us in the back. 😉

gertrude

DO NOT make puns right now.

claudius

Oh come on. It's a layup.

gertrude

I mean it. I'm not in the mood.

Send

Group text: Claudius, Rosencrantz, Guildenstern

claudius

I need u 2 get help ASAP. Hamlet has killed Polonius. Find Hamlet & bring the body 2 the 🏛. NOW!!!

[Scene 2]

Group text: Rosencrantz, Guildenstern, Hamlet

rosencrantz

What have u done w/ the body?

Hamlet

It's where it belongs.

rosencrantz

It belongs in the 🏛. Tell us!!!!

Hamlet

Why should I tell you anything? You're just a pawn of the king. He takes what he wants, and then he disposes of you when he's done.

rosencrantz

IDK what you're talking about.

Send

Hamlet

THAT I believe.

[Scene 3]

Group text: Rosencrantz, Guildenstern, Claudius

Rosencrantz

He won't tell us anything.

Guildenstern

He's just playing games.

Claudius

WHERE IS POLONIUS?

Hamlet

At supper.

Claudius

Huh?

Send

Hamlet

Well, *he's* not eating, exactly.

Cuz he's in the ground. #worms 🐛🐛🐛

claudius

WHERE IS POLONIUS?!?!?!?!

Hamlet

With the 🍽️🍽️. Check heaven, and if he's not there, then you'll know where to find him. 🔥😈🔥

claudius

That's it. I'm gonna drop u from the 👨‍👩‍👧 plan.

Hamlet

Wait! If you want to 👃 him out (heh heh), look under ⬇️ the stairs on the way 2 the lobby.

Group text: Claudius, Hamlet, Rosencrantz, Guildenstern

claudius

👀 under the stairs near the lobby.

Send

Hamlet

No rush, fellas. He's not going anywhere.

claudius

Enough is enough. 😤 You're going 2 🇬🇧 . NOW.

Hamlet

Fine. I'll go to 🇬🇧 . NOW. Whatever, 👸 .

claudius

It's official. You've gone bat 💩 crzy. I'm your father. 👨
Not your mother. 👸

Hamlet

👨 + 👸 + ⛪ = same flesh, right?

So 👨 = 👸 . You can't fight logic!

claudius

"Logic" isn't the word I'd use.

Send

CLAUDIUS

BACK · **CLAUDIUS** · +

To Do:

1. Have the 👑 of 🇬🇧 kill Hamlet.

2. Upload more selfies on throne.

Hmm. Light day.

Group text: Claudius, Rosencrantz, Guildenstern

claudius

> FYI, I left a ✉ 4 u 2 bring on your trip. It's addressed 2 the 👑 of 🇬🇧. Hurry!

[Scene 4]

BACK · **HAMLET** · +

Just saw a captain in Fortinbras's army. The poor guy is going to fight—and probably DIE—over a piece of land no one even cares about!! Ugh. What is the point of a man if all

Send

he ever does is ₂z^Z and 🍴 ? That's no better than 🐶 🐱 🐷 🐼 . My father's dead. My mother's dead to me. From now on, I'm going to stop thinking so much and just do the thing I set out to do. No excuses. 🚫

[Scene 5]

Horatio

> Your Majesty, I think you need to talk to Ophelia.

Gertrude

> Why me?

Horatio

> She's 😫. She's not making any sense. She's gone 🌀 over the death of her father.

> Seems to be a trend. ✓

Gertrude

> Sigh. Fine.

Send

Group text: Gertrude, Ophelia, Claudius

gertrude

Hello, Ophelia.

ophelia

gertrude

Ophelia, please. I don't understand.

ophelia

gertrude

Ophelia. Please use your words.

ophelia

claudius

How are you, Ophelia?

ophelia

Send

claudius

Is this because of your father?

ophelia

✕ ✕ ✕

claudius

Wut's going on?

ophelia

claudius

Uh, we'll get back 2 u.

Group text: Claudius, Horatio, Gertrude

claudius

Yikes! Horatio, follow Ophelia! & keep  over her! She has completely lost it, Hamlet-style. 🌀 w/ 👁 over Polonius.

Send

gertrude

Do you hear something? It sounds like someone has broken into the 🏰?!

claudius

There's a huge angry mob 😠😠😠 outside!!! They are shouting: "Laertes shall be 👑!!" 📢

✅ Laertes has checked into Elsinore Castle—with Huge Angry Mob.

👍 Huge Angry Mob likes this

Group text: Laertes, Claudius, Gertrude

Laertes

CLAUDIUS!!!! U MUST SPEAK W/ ME @ ONCE!!!! I WILL CALL OFF MY HUGE ANGRY MOB BUT ONLY IF U SPEAK W/ ME NOW!!!!!!

claudius

Wut would u like 2 discuss?

Laertes

WHERE IS MY FATHER?

Send

claudius

😵

gertrude

But we didn't kill him!

Laertes

THEN WHO DID?!?! TELL ME!! I WILL NOT SPARE U UNLESS U TELL ME EXACTLY WHAT HAPPENED. I DON'T CARE THAT U R THE !!!! I WILL AVENGE HIS MURDER NOW!!!!!

claudius

I understand that u r upset. But calm down & we'll talk!! I'm 😡 & 😭 that Polonius is 😵 2!!

● ● ●

Laertes

Ophelia!! My sweet sister. Where r u?

ophelia

Send

Laertes

NO NO NO NO NO

ophelia

Laertes

DON'T TELL ME U R AS 😵 2 THE 🌎 AS DAD!!

ophelia

Laertes

U demanding revenge would not make me as 😡 as seeing u 🌀 like this!

ophelia

Laertes

DEAR GOD, WUT HAPPENED 2 OPHELIA?!?!

Send

claudius

Look. U can literally ask any1 in the entire 🏰 . Every1 will tell u Gert and I had nuthin 2 do w/ it. U can have my 👑 & 🏰 if any1 tells u otherwise. K?

Laertes

Fine. But the way he 😵 and the way u guys buried him was BS. No ⛪️ 🐝 or anything. Someone's gonna pay, man.

claudius

I know. But find out wut actually happened b4 u jump 2 conclusions. And then u can get revenge. K?

Laertes

Fine.

Send

[Scene 6]

 Welcome, Horatio! You have 1 new message from Hamlet.

Horatio,

We were only out to for 2 days when our ⛵ was overtaken by pirates. They took me as their prisoner, and while they've been decent so far, they want me to do them a favor. R&G are still on their way to 🇬🇧. I have so much to tell you but it will have to be later. Find me ASAP!

Yours,

Hamlet

PS: See attached for some letters to the 👑.

 King1.doc
📎 King2.doc

[Scene 7]

claudius

> Did u ask ppl yet?

Send

Laertes

Yes.

claudius

So u know I didn't do n-e-thing wrong. & in fact Hamlet was trying 2 🔪 me?!?! #RegicideAmIRight

Laertes

I guess, but u still should have done something about it!!!!

claudius

Wut do u want me 2 do??

1. I'm married 2 Hamlet's mother, remember?? 👩‍❤️‍👨

2. U know how ppl 💜 him around here. They think he is an 🎩 ! N-e-thing I say will only make me look bad.

Laertes

So wut am I supposed 2 do?! My dad is . My sister's 🌀. I must get revenge somehow.

claudius

I have a plan in the works but u gotta b patient. BRB.

Send

📫 Welcome, Claudius! You have 1 new message from Hamlet.

> High & mighty, I'm coming back to Denmark. Alone.
> I will apologize and explain everything to you
> tomorrow.
>
> Claudius ➡️ 📧 Laertes

claudius

Check ur 📥. I just forwarded u something.

Laertes

Is that really from Hamlet??

claudius

It says "Sent from Hamlet's iPhone." Why is he alone??

Laertes

IDK but let him come. 💩 is about 2 get real.

claudius

Can I help?

Send

Laertes

Yeah, as long as u don't try 2 convince me 2 💋 and 💄 .

claudius

Why would I tell u 2 wear 💄 ?

Laertes

*make up

claudius

No, I want u 2 get ur revenge!! I have a plan that will make it seem like an accident. That way, Gertrude won't get 😡 & we can continue 2 live 2gether in sin. Lolz.

Laertes

I don't care wut happens as long as I get 2 🗡 Hamlet myself.

claudius

Def.

Laertes

So wut's the plan?

Send

claudius

Ur still pretty awesome @ fencing, right?

Laertes

Yeah.

claudius

OK, so u challenge Hamlet 2 a fencing duel when he gets back. But instead of using a blunted blade . . .

Laertes

I'LL POISON THE TIP OF MY SWORD!!!!

claudius

I was just going 2 say u use a real sword.

But poison works 2. lol

Laertes

We should have a backup plan in case sumthing goes wrong.

claudius

Yeah ur rite. 💡 Let's have 🍷 filled with poison 2!

Send

claudius

But rly, wut could go wrong?!?!

Group text: Gertrude, Claudius, Laertes

Gertrude

I need to speak with you both ASAP.

claudius

1 sec. We're in the middle of something.

Gertrude

We have to talk NOW.

claudius

Wut?

Gertrude

⚠ More bad news. Laertes . . .

Laertes

What?

WHAT?!

Send

Gertrude

IDK how 2 say this . . . your sister has drowned. 😭

Laertes

OH 💩 ! OPHELIA? WHERE? HOW?

Gertrude

There is a willow down by the river. She was collecting 🌼 🌻 🌹 and making them into garlands. She fell into the 🌊 , and for a ⏳ her 👗 held her up. But then the 💧 became too heavy and pulled her down.

I'm so sorry.

Laertes

I cannot even 😭 because there's 2 much 💧 already. G2G

👤 Claudius

Rly glad I just wasted a lot of ⏰ & energy talking someone down. FML

👍 REPLY

Send

Act 5

[Scene 1]

☑ Hamlet and Horatio have checked into the Church Graveyard.

 Gravedigger
Digging a grave in the cemetery, but IDK why bc this person took their own life. #MoneyTalks

                                    REPLY

Hamlet: Whose grave is it?
Gravedigger: Mine.
Hamlet: What 🔼 are you digging this for?
Gravedigger: No man.
Hamlet: Then what 🔼?
Gravedigger: None.
Hamlet: SMH. Who is going to be BURIED here?
Gravedigger: She WAS a woman. But now she's no one.
Hamlet: I guess that's how it goes. Life, ya know? 😃 then 💀.

☑ Gertrude, Claudius, Laertes, and a Priest have checked into the Church Graveyard.

                                    Send

Hamlet

Horatio, did you see who just checked in?

Horatio

Yeah. What should we do?

Hamlet

Let's ⌚, but keep our distance.

I see a casket. But it's weird to have such a small funeral.

Horatio

Can you 👂 what they're saying?

Hamlet

⚠ ⚠ ⚠ They are talking about Ophelia!!!
OMG Ophelia is DEAD?!

Horatio

I'm so sorry. 😭

Hamlet

It can't be! And yet Laertes just keeps going on and on about how 😔 he is. Doesn't he know I 😍 her, too?!

Send

Hamlet

Laertes, is it true? Ophelia is ?! I loved her w/ all my 🖤!

Laertes

Well, I loved her more! 🖤🖤

Hamlet

Oh, really? 🖤🖤🖤

Laertes

🖤 x infinity

Hamlet

This is ridiculous. I'm not going to fight with you over who loved her more. (Me.)

Laertes

cough Me. Also bc u know u will lose.

Hamlet

Screw you.

Laertes

And 😈 take you!

Send

[Scene 2]

Hamlet

Laertes is such a 🔧.

Horatio

Lol

Hamlet

Oh! I still have to tell you about the thing!

Horatio

That's right! Can you tell me now?

Hamlet

Yes. So when I was traveling with R&G, I had this gut feeling that something was wrong. I decided to steal the ✉ Claudius had given them, just to see what it said. 😏 Well, I'm hella glad I did because I found out . . .

Horatio

YES?! What did you find out?

Send

Hamlet

He had given the 👑 of 🇬🇧 instructions to 🗡 ME.

Horatio

OH HELL NO. Claudius did that?!

Hamlet

See for yourself if you want. I still have the ✉.

Horatio

What did you do???

Hamlet

I re 📝 the ✉ except this time, I said to 🗡 Rosencrantz & Guildenstern. I used the Denmark royal seal and everything. #BWAHAHAHA

Horatio

So R&G are now & .

Hamlet

Self-defense!

Send

Horatio

You know Claudius is going to find out what happened.

Hamlet

Which is why I have to act quickly.

I do feel bad that I yelled at Laertes, though. We're basically in the same . I'll be nice to him from now on.

Claudius

@Hamlet @Laertes: I challenge u 2 a duel! Place your bets, ladies & gentlemen. Winner gets #SWAG #SWAG #SWAG #SWAG

👍   REPLY

Laertes: Come @ me bro
Hamlet: *shrug* Why not?
Horatio: You guys sure this is a good idea?
Gertrude: How early is too early to start drinking?

Send

Hamlet

> Laertes, we should talk before the duel.

Laertes

> I'm listening.

Hamlet

> I'm sorry for what I said. I'm sorry about your dad and your sister. I shouldn't have been such a 👶.
> We actually have a lot in common, you & me.

Laertes

> Thx. I need ⏰ 2 think about everything, but I appreciate ur text.

✅ Hamlet, Horatio, Laertes, Claudius, and Gertrude have checked into the Elsinore Castle Lobby.

 Horatio
Hello, and welcome to the @Laertes @Hamlet "Elsinore Castle Throwdown." I will be live-posting events as they happen. 👊 💥

👍

REPLY

Claudius: Let's get this started!!!

Send

Horatio

+1 for @Hamlet!

👍 REPLY

Claudius: I'll drink to that. Good work, son!

Gertrude: Save some 🍷 for me. 😉

 Horatio

+1 again for @Hamlet. I thought @Laertes was the swordsman? #Rumors #2Good2BTrue

👍 REPLY

Gertrude: Cheers, @Hamlet! 🙌 I drink to your health!

Claudius: NO! @Gertrude! Do NOT drink that wine.

Gertrude: Too late! #NomNomNom

Send

Horatio

+1 for @Laertes! It looks like he's drawn blood from @Hamlet's shoulder!! 🗡 Is he using a real sword?! #CheaterCheater

👍   REPLY

Crowd: Booooo!

 Horatio

Okay, well, now @Laertes and @Hamlet are just 👊💥👊💥. This is some crazy 💩.

👍   REPLY

 Horatio

What's this? @Hamlet and @Laertes have accidentally switched swords! Well, we've never seen this before, folks, nor are we likely to see it again!

👍   REPLY

Crowd: We're getting our 💰💰 worth!

Send

Horatio
The Queen has collapsed in the stands! Someone call the !! Wait, I'm on my 📱. *facepalm* Hold on. . . .

👍 | REPLY |

Group text: Hamlet, Laertes, Claudius, Gertrude

Hamlet

⏰ OUT! Laertes needs help.

Laertes

Hamlet, we've been poisoned by my sword. There's no antidote on 🌍. We r both about 2 😵. I'm ✒ by my own treachery. #MyBad

But rly it's all 👉 Claudius's fault!!!

Claudius

Who, me?! 😇

Hamlet

Mom! What's wrong?

Send

claudius

She fainted at the sight of u & Laertes bleeding.

Gertrude

No. It was the 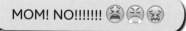. Hamlet, I've been poisoned!

Hamlet

MOM! NO!!!!!!! 😫😖😣

 Horatio

@Laertes is dying right before our 👀. And OMG! @Hamlet has stopped fencing and is forcing the poisoned down @Claudius's throat! Now he's stabbed the 👑!!

👍   REPLY

Crowd: Treason!!! 👎
Horatio: The king and queen are now . 🚓
Crowd: *gasp*

Hamlet

Laertes

Hamlet, dude, I'm so sry. Do u forgive me?
I forgive u. It was all Claudius.

Hamlet

On that we can agree.

We're cool. Die in 🖐.

✅ Fortinbras has checked into Elsinore Castle—with 10,000 others.

Hamlet

I'm dying, Horatio.

Horatio

NO. Hamlet. Stay away from the 💡!

Send

Hamlet

There's not much ⏳. My hands are growing too weak to type. You are the only one who can tell the real 📖 now. My dad, Gertrude, Claudius, Laertes, Polonius, and Ophelia. All dead and gone. #RIP #ExceptClaudius

Horatio

Hamlet, I can't. I'll drink the poison, too! ⚡ \

Hamlet

NO. ✖ Horatio, listen. Not only does someone need to clean up all these bodies, but you're the only one left who knows the truth. Promise me you'll tell everyone everything (especially Fortinbras). Even if it means living longer in this awful 🌍. Please. Remember me. 👬

Horatio

I will, always. May the take you to a better place.

Send

Fortinbras

Oh, HELL NO. What the WHAT?!?!
#SoManyBodies

👍   REPLY

Horatio: It's a long . Let's talk IRL.
Fortinbras: Sure thing, bro. In the mean ,
prepare a hero's burial for Hamlet. I hear he
was a good egg. 🔍 Scrambled, but good.

👍 Angry Mob likes this

Send

The 411 for Those Not in the Know

411: Information

ASAP: As Soon As Possible

BFF: Best Friend Forever

BRB: Be Right Back

BTW: By The Way

FML: F*ck My Life

FOMO: Fear Of Missing Out

FTW: For The Win

FYI: For Your Information

G2G: Got To Go

IDK: I Don't Know

ILY: I Love You

IMHO: In My Humble Opinion

IRL: In Real Life

LMK: Let Me Know

LOL: Laughing Out Loud

Send

LOLZ: Lots of Laughs

NBD: No Big Deal

NP: No Problem

OIC: Oh I See

OMG: Oh My God

SMH: Shaking My Head

TL;DR: Too Long; Didn't Read

TTYL: Talk To You Later

WTF: What The F*ck

YOLO: You Only Live Once

Send

some emotions you might find in this book

😠 Angry

😣 Anguished

😅 Anxious

😖 Confounded

🙁 Confused

😎 Cool

😵 Dead/Dying

😞 Disappointed

😊 Embarrassed (and/or Drunk)

😈 Evil (Devil)

😘 Flirty

😉 Friendly (wink, wink)

😤 Fuming Mad

😜 Goofy

😃 Happy

Send

	Innocent
😍	Love
😰	Nervous
😑	Nothing
😡	Really Angry
😔	Sad
😭	Sad (and Crying)
😱	Scared
😬	Sheepish/Grimacing
😨	Shocked
😷	Sick
😶	Silent
😛	Silly
😴	Sleepy
😏	Sly
😳	Surprised
😒	Unamused
😦	Worried

Send

COURTNEY CARBONE studied English and creative writing in Baltimore, before moving to New York City to become a full-time children's book editor. When she isn't collaborating with the greatest playwright of all time, Courtney can be found studying various forms of comedy and trying to finish the joke, "Two groundlings walk into a bard. . . ." 👯

WILLIAM SHAKESPEARE was born in Stratford-upon-Avon in 1564. He was an English poet, playwright, and actor, widely regarded as the greatest writer in the English language and the world's preeminent dramatist. His plays have been translated into every major language and are performed more often than those of any other playwright. 🎭

Send

FOMO?

Read on for a peek at

romeo. 😊 romeo. 😊 ugh, why does he have to be a montague? i wish he'd just change his name. or if he said he'll 💜 me forever, then i'd give up my last name. c-ya, capulet! 🚫 what's the point of names anyway? srsly. you could call a 🌹 a different name, and it would still 👃 just as sweet. grr. stop being a montague and we can be together, romeo! 👫 that's 💯 better than anything else.

Send

Voice Memo from Romeo

I totally get what she's saying. I just need to
know that I'm her one true 💔 . Then I'll
drop ⬇️ Montague like a bad habit. 🚭

juliet

wait, romeo, is that you? 😦 have you been 👂 to
me this whole time?

Romeo

Maaaybe.

I want to show my face, but I know I shouldn't.
Because I'm a Montague. 😖

juliet

no, keep texting. it's easier this way. you're too far down.

i don't want my family to 👂 you yelling. they'll be
srsly upset. i'm talking, like, pissed. 😡

Send

how did you even get here? the walls around here are really high.

ROMEO

I scaled them, NBD. I couldn't wait to see you again!

And I'm not afraid of your family.

juliet

you should be. if they see you here, they'll kill you! 🔫

ROMEO

So what? That's nothing compared to being rejected by you. Chill. ❄️

juliet

sorry, it's just . . . i'd do anything to make sure they don't catch you.

ROMEO

Hello. I'm hidden in the dark. 🏙️ Plus, if you're not into me after all, then I'd rather be dead.

I can't live without you!

Send

juliet

srsly, how did you know where my bedroom was?

ROMEO

I just followed my 🖤. It led the way.

juliet

it's a good thing it's dark. you're making me blush.

listen, romeo. i really, really like you. i know I should have played hard-to-get, but i guess it's too late for that.

you heard me just now. i'm so into you. i mean . . .

i 🖤 you, romeo.

ROMEO

Juliet, I swear on the 🌙.

juliet

you swear on a piece of rock in the sky? um.

but the moon always changes. 🌙 🌑 🌕

Send

ROMEO

What should I swear on then?

juliet

maybe we shouldn't make any promises yet. all of this happened as fast as ⚡.

we have a good thing going. 👍 let's see what happens the next time we meet.

i'm gonna go now. zzZ hope you sleep as well as i plan to. 😃

ROMEO

You're leaving me already??

juliet

what else is there to say?

ROMEO

For starters, I'd be happy if we promised to 💜 each other forever. I'm talking, like, making it real. Like, married real.

Send

juliet

i've already poured my ♥ out to you. i'd take it back if i could.

ROMEO

What the duck, Juliet!

The duck.

Ugh! Autocorrect. 😑

juliet

heehee. quack, quack. 🐤

ROMEO

WTF Juliet. Why would you say that ⁉️

juliet

i'm just teasing. i mean i'd take it back so i could give it to you again and again. 😊 😉

i love you as deep as the ocean. 🌊 but i think i hear someone calling for me. hold on a sec. brb.

Send

Romeo
I wanna pinch myself. Am I dreaming or is this
happening IRL? #truluv #blessed

👍   REPLY

juliet

okay, romeo. real quick. if you really, truly 🖤 me and
want to get married . . .

let's chat tomorrow. sleep on it. we can figure out when
and where to get married. but only if you really mean it.

sweet dreams!

what time 🕐 should i text you tomorrow?

Romeo

Let's say 9. 🕐

juliet

perf! it's going to feel like years until then. 📅17

sorry i keep saying goodbye and then texting you again.
i had a reason this time, i swear. i just forget.

Send

Romeo

😃 That's okay. I'll stick around until you remember.

Juliet

in that case, it might take me forever to remember what it was. hmm . . .

Romeo

NP. Guess I found my new home right here.

Juliet

i wish you didn't have to go.

but the sooner we go to bed, the sooner it's tomorrow. g'night! 😘

Romeo

Sweet dreams, you.

🎵 Juliet is listening to Taylor Swift's "Love Story" on Renaissance FM

Send